Disney

BIG HERO 6

TEAM-UP!

By Laura Hitchcock
Illustrated by the Disney Storybook Art Team

A Random House PICTUREBACK® Book

Random House 🏠 New York

randomhousekids.com
ISBN 978-0-7364-3244-3
Printed in the United States of America
10 9 8 7 6 5 4 3 2 1

. . . Hiro. Hard to tell from looking at him, but this kid is a **ROBOTICS GENIUS**. One day, his inventions will change the world!

Hiro has a nurse-bot named Baymax.
He takes care of us and is super helpful.
But I was the one who suggested we
should all team up!

OUR TEAM
COULD BENEFIT FROM
SOME UPGRADES.

Hiro wasted no time. He created all kinds of tech stuff for each of us, based on our unique **strengths** and **talents**.

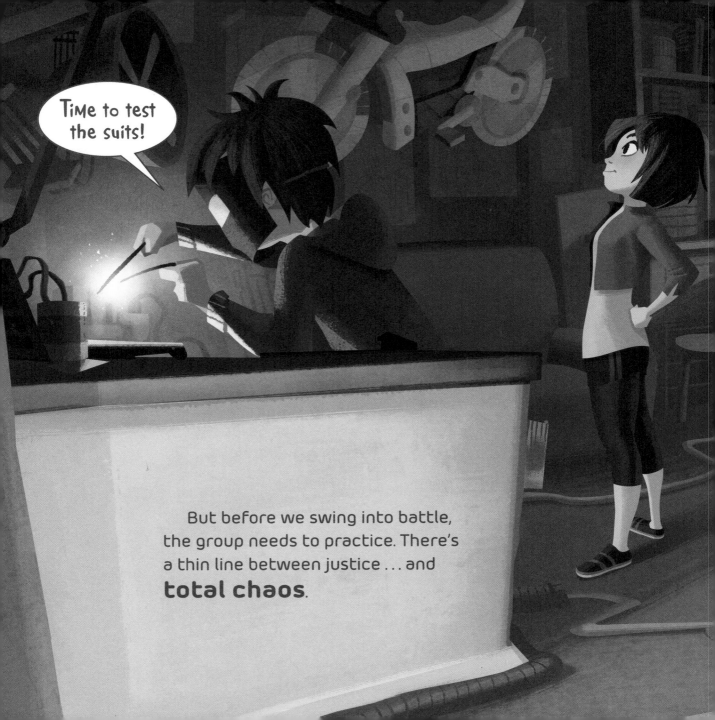

Honey Lemon is a master of chemistry.
Her purse is packed with chemicals that can be combined
to create all sorts of wacky weapons, like this super-sticky
foam that stops villains in their tracks!

Go Go Tomago's super suit has cool discs she can race on—after she practices a bit more! The discs can also be used as weapons—**they're razor-sharp**.

Baymax also has a powerful
rocket fist!

Hiro saved the best for last.
He gave me this amazing suit!

Villains, beware! Evil doesn't stand a chance against us. **We are Big Hero 6!**